The Village Idiots

Part 2 – Fool's Gold

Sara Alexi is the author of the Greek Village Series and the Greek Island Series

.

She divides her time between England and a small village in Greece.

http://facebook.com/authorsaraalexi

GW00503165

Sara Alexi

THE VILLAGE IDIOTS

Part 2 – Fool's Gold

oneiro

Published by Oneiro Press 2017

ISBN: 9781549649783

Also by Sara Alexi

Chapter 1

'But how can you be sure the gold is on the boat?' Takis asks Babis. He speaks in a low whisper, looking around him to make sure the other villagers in the *kafenio* are not listening. Spiros pulls his chair closer to the table, grimacing as the legs scrape noisily on the floor. Takis obviously does not want to attract any attention. But the farmers in the café are huddled in groups around their tables, drinking coffees and ouzos, focused on their own thoughts, playing *tavli*, discussing football, farming or politics.

Outside the floor-to-ceiling windows there's a dark-skinned man in African dress, with a tray hung on a strap around his neck. He mounts the three steps up to the *kafenio* and looks in tentatively. Spiros does not look away in time and the man catches his eye, then enters, casually and slowly. But his eyes betray him, glancing one way and the other, before he fixes his gaze on Theo, the owner. He sneaks across to Spiros's table, trying not to attract Theo's attention.

'What can I interest you in?'

His accent is thick and he is hard to understand. His worn sandals click-slap on the concrete floor. The straps are broken and he slides his feet to keep the sandals on. There are holes in his trousers but his shirt is brightly coloured with a geometric pattern.

Takis and Babis stop talking as he approaches the table, sitting back in their chairs and staring at the tall stranger. The African has all the time in the world; his languid fingers pick out a pair of sunglasses from his tray.

'Glasses, my friend? Ray-Ban, the real thing.'

Spiros tries to think of a way to ask him to leave but without being rude.

'Torch? Very good. Waterproof. You want?'

Spiros opens his mouth to say no, thank you and good day, when Takis leans over.

'Go,' he says simply, looking the man in the eye.

Theo comes over too. 'Come on, now, my friend. Let's be having you.'

Theo guides the man as if herding a sheep, and the man, with his thick accent and worn shoes, turns without a word and shuffles out. Theo goes back behind his counter. Babis watches the man as he crosses the road and sits on the bench opposite, then he turns back to Takis.

'The gold must be on the boat. George had nowhere else to put it. He had no house, no *apothiki*, no close friends – not that close, anyway – and as we know, no relations, so the gold must be on the boat.'

'Where?' Takis presses him.

'It's not clear, but it's only a boat, a finite area to search. How many cupboards and lockers can there be?'

'Actually,' Spiros speaks up, 'under the cushions are lockers, and under the lockers are boards that lift up, and there are spaces underneath. I saw it when we went out to the island.'

4

'Yes,' Takis agrees. 'If George was so smart, there are hundreds of little nooks he could have stashed the gold in.'

'Yes, but that is my point. Hundreds, not thousands, not infinite,' Babis says.

Spiros watches the African man, who crosses the road slowly, sits on the bench in the shade of the palm tree. He arranges his sunglasses on his tray, lining them up carefully. Babis stands to leave.

'Well, there you have it, boys. Let me know how you want to proceed.' Babis stands and stretches, drinks the last of his coffee and walks out, nodding to Cosmo the postman, who is just coming in.

'How on earth are we going to get the gold?' Spiros asks. 'The boat is at the bottom of the harbour.'

'Hi, guys.' Cosmo comes over to their table. Takis scowls.

'Can I join you?' Cosmo asks, and he moves to sit down without waiting for an answer. Takis grunts, but Spiros speaks first.

'Hi, Cosmo, of course.' He helps draw back the chair for the postman. Takis glares at him.

'Morning, Cosmo.' Theo wanders over to them. 'What can I get you?'

'I'll have a – oh, damn.' He stands more quickly than he sat and picks up his postal sack from where he dumped it by his chair.

'What is it?' Theo asks, putting his hands on his hips and looking across the square, watching the man with the tray of torches and sunglasses, who is now talking to Vasso in the kiosk.

'I said I would feed Poppy's cat.' Cosmo slings the bag over his shoulder. 'You would not believe what sort of day I have had! I was really looking forward to sitting for a few minutes with a coffee. Oh well.'

'We'll go and feed the cat for you,' Takis says, and the others all turn to stare at him.

'Are you sure?' Cosmo says, not sounding at all sure himself. But then he hesitates – a hope has been ignited, and his weariness seems quickly to compel him to retake his seat.

'If it's no trouble …' he says, taking a key from his pocket.

'Sure, me and Spiros will go. You take a break and then finish your work.' Takis sounds very friendly, and Spiros searches his friend's face to try to understand what is going on. Takis does not even like cats.

It is only when they are outside that Spiros realises they have not paid for their coffees.

'Did you say you would feed his neighbour's cat to get him to pay for the coffees?' he asks, looking back.

'Damn the cat, this is Poppy's shop we are talking about.'

Spiros has always loved Poppy's shop. It is unlike any other in the village, or in Saros, come to that. She sells old things that are no longer wanted – colourful tank tops that were hand-knitted with care but never got to be worn, and wrap-around trousers whose days of being in fashion had long gone even by the time Poppy acquired them. The smell of mothballs usually lingers over the second-hand stock. Once, he recalls, there was a designer suit in the window, a useless thing for any farmer's wife.

'If we are not feeding the cat, then what?' Spiros asks as they cross the square and start up the side street that leads to Poppy's shop. Takis jangles the keys but doesn't answer. He strides purposefully up the lane, leaving Spiros to hurry after him.

He twists the key in the lock and the heat rushes out of the door at them, bringing with it a smell of mothballs and old wool. It reminds Spiros of his proyiayia's sewing box, which was packed with darning thread and crochet needles and an assortment of buttons.

'Do you know where the cat food is kept?' Spiros looks around for the cat.

'No idea,' Takis says, striding over to the counter at the back of the shop. Spiros looks over to see what he is doing, and his heart misses a beat when he sees Takis standing facing a very tall man with a large head. It takes a moment for him to realise that the other man is really an old-fashioned deep-sea diving suit.

'Here, give me a hand,' Takis demands as he lifts the big brass helmet to reveal a mannequin inside.

Without the support of the helmet, the suit crumples to the floor. Takis puts the helmet on the counter and gathers up the rubber suit, folding in the arms and legs and rolling it up.

'Oh, look,' he says, taking a torch out of a box on the counter, 'aren't these like the ones that man was

7

selling? Waterproof, he said.' He stuffs the torch in his pocket. 'Come on, then.'

Spiros picks up the suit. It is made of a strange rubbery material and is quite heavy.

'But Taki, we have no money to pay for this, and Poppy is not here anyway.'

'We'll just borrow it.'

'We didn't ask.' Memories of taking Mitsos's truck return, from when they sank the boat in the first place for the insurance money that didn't exist. 'But Taki …'

'We borrow it, we use it, no one gets hurt and no one is the wiser,' Takis says as if it is common sense, a matter of fact. 'Come on, let's go.'

'But we need to feed the cat,' Spiros says.

'Later – we'll feed her later. Right now we need to get this down to the jetty. If we stash it under the top end with the nets, then later, when it gets dark, we can go and try it out.'

Spiros knows what Takis means when he says 'we' will try it out. It won't be Takis in the water in the antique suit.

'What if we are seen? It's still half light out there.'

'Well, we can't wait here,' Takis urges him. 'We have to risk it. Look, with it all rolled up, no one will know what it is anyway.'

Spiros picks up the big brass helmet.

'You can't roll this up.'

'Well, you can't take it like that. Here.' Takis throws a pair of trousers at him. 'Cover it with them.'

Spiros does the best he can, but the helmet is big and the trousers will not cover it completely.

'Go through the orange trees,' Takis says. 'I'll lock up and meet you there.'

Spiros's heart pounds as he leaves the shop. What if Cosmo is around the corner? He walks quickly and ducks down the lane that leads to the orange grove, his heart almost bursting through his ribcage by the time he is safely under the trees. He takes a moment, leaning back against the trunk of one of the orange trees to catch his breath and let his heartbeat slow down.

'Come on, then.' Takis catches him up with easy long strides.

'Taki, I'm really not sure this is right. I mean, if we are hiding our actions then they can't be good, can they?' Spiros says.

'Stop making a fuss. It's not as if Poppy would mind. She's had this thing so long she would probably be glad someone was putting it to good use.'

They take the long way through the orange groves, avoiding the little cottage at its centre and skirting past the back of Stella's hotel, towards the beach. Spiros recalls that large items of furniture used to be dumped here, and there were often rusting fridges and old sofas marring the otherwise idyllic view of the bay. There's no rubbish here now, and instead trees have been planted and benches erected, presumably by Stella. The grass has yellowed with the summer sun, but nevertheless it is now a lovely spot.

'Come on,' Takis pulls at his sleeve, and Spiros fumbles with the big round helmet. The thing is heavy and slippery, wrapped up in the trousers, and he folds his arm more firmly around it.

By the time they get to the outer edge of the grove and onto the beach the light is fading fast.

'Okay, so I don't suppose there'll be anyone down here now,' Takis says.

'What about night fishers?' Spiros looks up and down the beach. The lights of Saros town twinkle in the distance.

'Thanasis is the only night fisher I know, and he's taken Poppy off for a few days, so we don't need to worry about him.'

Takis unrolls the suit on the jetty and folds out the arms and legs, pressing them down with his hand. It looks like a flat cartoon man lying there.

'Right, come on, put the helmet down and in you get,' he says.

'I don't understand what the suit is for. I can swim, you know.'

'Yes, but you'll be down there for a while when we come to the real thing, and the window in the helmet will give you good vision.'

'But if it's heavy it will ...'

'It will keep you on the bottom, so you can search for longer.'

'But it might keep me down when I need to come up to breathe.'

'Ah, yes, we need a tube.'

10

Takis begins to hunt amongst the debris under the jetty, sorting through nets and buckets until, with an 'Aha!', he pulls free a length of hose.

'Perfect. So if we attach this to the nozzle at the back of the helmet it will fill with air while you are down there and you can breathe as normal,' he says with authority.

Spiros is not sure why, but he feels it won't be this easy. He begins to wriggle into the unwieldy suit and is sweating by the time he is in. He pushes the gloves over his hands and Takis fastens them. Once the suit is adjusted to sit well, Takis puts the brass collar over Spiros's head and starts twisting the little brass wing nuts, tighter and tighter, sealing the suit to the chest plate.

Then he lowers the big brass helmet over Spiros's head and works at twisting it into a locked position. It finally attaches to the collar with a satisfying clunk, and the little circular windows in the helmet immediately fog up.

It's difficult to see anything or hear Takis's instructions. Spiros thinks Takis is holding the tube up and then he feels something touch him on the back of the head; Takis must be feeding the tube in through the hole at the back, and with a suddenness that startles him the tube appears by his left eye and then pokes him on the bridge of his nose.

'Oi!' Spiros shouts, and Takis pulls at the helmet and looks through the window.

'Ah, it's there,' he says, and he produces a roll of tape from somewhere, and Spiros listens as metres of the stuff are wrapped, presumably, around the tube where it enters the suit at the back. 'Okay, you're ready.'

11

'And why are we doing this in the dark?' Spiros feels the need to shout to make himself heard through the heavy brass helmet.

'Because when we do this for real it will have to be at night. We don't want the world asking why we are diving, do we? The gold has to be kept a secret, else we are asking for trouble.'

He pauses and looks through the little window, his face so close Spiros can see the blackheads on his nose and a lone hair poking from one nostril. Flecks of spit land on the outside of the little window as he speaks.

Takis slaps the back of the helmet and it reverberates uncomfortably, and Spiros responds by trying to take a step towards the jetty. The boots are heavy and it takes all his concentration to walk in a straight line. The metal soles land heavily on the wooden treads and the noise resounds inside his dome. It is unbearably warm in the suit. Despite the breathing tube, the air smells stale.

'I don't want to jump in,' he says as he nears the end of the jetty.

'What?' Takis shouts, and he presses his ear against the glass window.

'I want to step into the water, climb down,' Spiros says.

'Here.'

He looks down to see that Takis has put the torch in his hand. Its strong beam creates a finger of light in the half gloom.

'Over there,' Takis says, and he leads him to a rickety set of steps that run from the end of the jetty down into the water.

Chapter 2

Spiros turns his back to the water and heads down the steps one rung at a time, holding on tight to the uprights of the ladder. Halfway in he can feel something cold in the back of the suit, water seeping in, dribbling down his leg. That shouldn't be happening, surely – but it's only his feet that are wet, and Takis will not be pleased if he comes up again.

The torch lights up long strands of seaweed, anchored to the steps, that snake slowly around his knees one way and then the other in the gloom. Below, the water is black and Spiros is not at all sure he wants to go any further in. This doesn't seem like a good idea after all. He tries to look up, but the helmet doesn't move with his head and only the inside of the brass dome is visible. Still only waist-deep in the water, he is finding the air stale and he wonders how much is coming through the hose.

Reluctantly he takes another three steps down. The water is up to his shoulders now; inside the suit the level has risen to his knees. As he descends another step and the helmet starts to submerge, Spiros experiences an odd mix of fear and curiosity. The surface bisects the little glass window, creating his own personal horizon: below this watery line he can see the rungs of the ladder and the seaweed, clearly illuminated by the torchlight; above it, Takis's face peers down at him, shining in the moonlight and surrounded by a halo of stars.

14

Another step and he is underwater. It is dark outside the circle of light cast by the torch. Spiros's heart has speeded up. The ink-black is his enemy, harbouring hostile creatures in its dark corners. He sucks in the stale air and grips the steps more tightly, and then, as if it is a gift from God, a brightly coloured fish swims past his window, its body wriggling back and forth, iridescent in the torch's beam. The beauty of it takes his whole attention, his breathing becomes calm and he feels he is the luckiest man in the world to have experienced such a sight.

He looks out for more fish but all he can see are the steps of the ladder in front of him and the leg of the jetty behind. He turns to look into the black and the suit resists. Another step down and he is rewarded by a shoal of coloured fish, with black eyes and a black stripe behind each head. Suddenly they dart in all directions, out of the beam of light. He wants to see more, but his focus returns to the deep midnight sea behind the fish and he takes in air in little gasps, trying to remain calm. In the torchlight he can just make out where the sea bottom rises to the surface and becomes black, presumably where the land meets the sea. The distance to dry land is not too great and this gives comfort. But why is it always he who has to do these things – why doesn't Takis ever take a turn?

Another fish darts past and again he feels privileged to be experiencing this sight. Another step down and   too late – he finds there is nothing but water under him and he begins to sink. His legs dangle below him, unnerving him, the weight of the suit dragging him down. Dropping the torch, he grabs with both hands for the steps, but the big gloves are awkward. He grips hard, fearing for his life. The water inside the suit is now above his waist and it is not warm. Focusing on the step, he tenses his biceps to pull himself up but the boots are too heavy. Is he is in danger? The water isn't deep here, he knows that, and Takis is above him. The dark lurks beneath his feet, but Takis will be displeased if he gives up.

He makes an effort to tuck his knee up against his chest, to try to get his foot on the step, but the action pulls him away from the seaweed-covered ladder, the green under his fingers slithers away and he is sinking … His breathing quickens and his lungs suck harder. His head swims slightly. The air tube has drooped and is nudging his mouth, which he opens to gulp more air, arms and legs flailing. He looks down but can only see the inside of the helmet. His breath quickens; he starts to wave his arms, clawing at the water. Blood rushes through his ears, and a scream begins to form in his chest, working its way up to his tight throat …

At last, he feels the seabed under his feet, and his panic subsides a little. The drop was not so great after all. In the gloom, as he leans back to look up, the moon's light silhouettes the rungs of the wooden ladder above. The rest is all dark, save a glow coming from under his feet somewhere – the fallen torch. Now the water inside the suit is up to his shoulders. That is definitely not meant to happen. The tube nudges his mouth again; he nibbles at it with his lips and draws it into his mouth. If the water rises much higher he will not be able to breathe without the tube. His heart begins to race again. Fish swim past, but his vision is fixed on the ladder, just out of reach, and they go by only half seen. He sucks heavily on the tube – the taste of stale plastic is fouler than the air in the helmet – but the air does not come, and the air in the helmet is making him dizzy now. He lifts his arms up to grab the bottom rung of the ladder, and tries to jump, but he can't reach it. In his sudden and overwhelming desire to get out of the water, his need for air made desperate by the knowledge that the tube is not functioning, he rushes the move; he misjudges it, and as he puts his foot down the ground is soft and slippery and his boot slides under him, behind him. He tips forward and the weight of the helmet pulls him headfirst, past the ladder and the jetty leg, to spiral to the ocean floor.

Cold water rushes over his face. His slow-moving hand grabs at the helmet but it will not come off. With a desperate struggle, he flips off one of the gloves and grabs at the helmet, but realises the futility of it, then flips off the other glove, and with both hands struggles with the wing nuts that attach the brass collar to the suit. He rolls onto his back and a pocket of air appears above his face; he takes a deep breath and holds the air in his lungs as he twists frantically at the next wing nut and then the next. How many were there? Another one is released, and the front of the collar starts to detach from the suit. He reaches behind his head; there are more there. Now the next one is off, and he stretches his hand behind his head, reaching desperately for the one after that. He can hold his breath a little longer, but he is not sure how long. Finally, with the last nut done, he pulls off the helmet and collar in one movement and squirms like an eel to rid himself of the suit. His need for air is desperate now. He works harder, and then, kicking his feet free, he pushes off the bottom and reaches for the surface, thrashing at the water with his hands. He kicks like a madman and pulls at the water until he bursts to the surface and gulps a great lungful of air.

Takis is there on the jetty, peering down at him, one hand extended. Spiros is a little distance from the pier now, though, and he needs more air. He sucks in another lungful and flaps his arms to propel him to the shadow of the jetty. The seaweed on the ladder feels so good in its slippery firmness, and with grateful legs he hauls himself up them and flings himself on the jetty, rolling onto his back.

'Where's the suit?' Takis asks.

Spiros coughs and spits to one side.

'You okay? What happened?'

'The tube didn't work, the suit let in water,' Spiros gasps.

'So you were down there with no air?' Takis helps him sit and pats his back.

Spiros nods and blinks. He feels dizzy but he has never been so glad to see the night sky, the shining moon, and to feel the solidity of the jetty beneath him.

'Christ, you can hold your breath!' Takis whistles through his teeth and peers over the edge of the jetty, down into the water. 'Well, we'd better get the suit, then, even if it is no good – take it back to Poppy's.'

'I nearly drowned!' Spiros's heart rate is slowing and he is no longer gasping for air.

'It's only three metres deep. You can't drown in three metres,' Takis scoffs. 'Right, well, seeing as you can hold your breath like a dolphin, best you dive in and get the suit back out.'

Takis turns back to him.

'No way!' Spiros says, more sharply than he intended.

'Well, unless you have another way of getting it back, or you want to explain to Poppy what you did …'

'What *I* did! It was your idea!' Spiros attempts to stand.

'Anyway, seeing as you can hold your breath so long, you can dive for the gold without a suit. You should have said. It would have saved us having to do all this.'

'I didn't know I could until I had to.' Spiros intends to sound indignant but it comes out like a whine.

'Right, in you go. No need to spend all night here.'

'No. I'm done.' Spiros runs his fingers through his hair, squeezing out the water.

'You want the gold, right? Well, this is good practice.'

Takis states this as if there is no choice, and Spiros feels his determination to remain on dry land wavering.

'Just think of the gold,' Takis continues. 'Imagine it glinting … Imagine us sitting and drinking coffee all day in Saros town like the rich folk!'

He laughs and Spiros feels drawn in, feels his will melting, and he looks down into the water, where he can see the glow of the torch on the seabed. It looks almost close enough to touch if he just reaches in.

'That's my boy, in you go.'

Spiros is about to say he is not a boy, and then Takis's arm is around his shoulder giving him a sideways hug, shoulder to shoulder, and he cannot help but smile. He takes another look over the edge.

'What lungs!' Takis says as if he is talking to himself, and this is the final encouragement Spiros needs to turn his back to the sea and start down the steps again.

The water covers his face but he has faith in his lungs now and he looks down at the pool of light cast by the torch beneath him. He lets go of the ladder and dives head first, and it only takes a couple of kicks to reach the bottom. He grips first the torch, and then the helmet and suit, but the two prove to be too heavy. A fish swims into the light and he stops to stare. His lungs feel strong; he could stay under longer. He holds onto the torch and the helmet and kicks his way up to the surface, handing the brass dome to Takis, who is face down on the jetty, waiting with arms outstretched. Spiros quite likes this game – as long as he doesn't think of what might be beyond the glow of the torch in the dark water. It takes two more dives to bring the whole suit up, and as he surfaces for the last time he grins triumphantly, hauling the brass collar up onto the jetty. Takis is holding up the suit.

'You've torn it!' he snaps.

'I nearly drowned!' Spiros's grin is wiped from his face.

'Well, we'll have to put it back and hope she doesn't notice.'

Takis rolls the suit and tucks it under his arm, and then takes the collar and puts it over his head, before starting to walk back along the jetty. Spiros grabs the helmet and runs to catch up, forgetting the wrap-around trousers in his haste. He remembers them when they reach the edge of the orange grove and has to run back for them, struggling to control his imagination under the dark trees.

In the village, no light glows from the windows, and no sounds can be heard except the barking of dogs, the evening chorus that will go on long into the night. Takis is extra quiet whilst opening Poppy's shop. The cat meows, and Spiros pets it whilst Takis arranges the diving suit on the mannequin.

'We need to feed the cat,' Spiros whispers.

'Tomorrow. We'll feed it tomorrow. Come on – if we're caught here now, we're done for.'

With this, Takis propels Spiros out through the front door, then locks it quietly behind them, and the two sneak like thieves back through the village, across the square and home to bed.

Chapter 3

Spiros wakes early the next morning, worrying that Poppy's cat will be feeling hungry and neglected. He scrambles into yesterday's clothes and, without a thought for his own breakfast, makes his way over to Takis's house, where he knocks, quietly, then tries the handle without waiting for an answer.

Thin curtains do their best to keep the early morning half-light out. The kitchen is a mirror image of Spiros's house, with a wooden table and four chairs in the middle, and one or two low cupboards against the walls. He tiptoes to the bedroom door, taps quietly so as not to disturb Takis if he is still asleep, and opens the door. Takis is snoring, a big misshapen lump under the covers in the single bed by the window; the air in the room is thick and stale. Light sneaks in through the crack in the shutters, which have not been fastened properly, and Spiros has no trouble making out where Takis discarded his trousers last night, slung over the back of a chair and trailing on the floor.

With the key to Poppy's shop in his hand he leaves Takis snoring, steps stealthily back into the fresh air and hurries down the lane, across the square and up to Poppy's before the first cockerel has sounded its raucous alarm.

The sun's first rays are breaking the horizon, lifting the grey blanket of night off the houses, to reveal the daytime orange of their terracotta roofs. Spiros looks about him, sees no one and quickly unlocks the door to the shop, before closing it quietly behind him. The cat is curled up asleep on Poppy's chair by the counter at the back of the shop, seemingly unconcerned that it has been callously abandoned. He strokes it behind its ears and it wakes, stretching and yawning, and begins an incessant mewing. Once on its feet, it jumps down and rubs itself up against the door frame at the back of the shop.

'Are you showing me the way?' Spiros asks, and he opens the door.

The animal trots down the corridor and through another door at the end, its tail held high. Spiros follows it through to the kitchen, where it then paws the door to the cupboard under the sink. There is a bowl on the floor for water, and one for food, both empty, but Spiros pauses for a minute to take in his surroundings: the standard wooden table, but with only two chairs, and pictures on the wall, photographs in black and white of severe-looking people from years gone by – no doubt long-dead relatives. At the far end, set in the opposite wall, is a glass-windowed doorway. Spiros is drawn to this door, through which he can see a tiny courtyard overflowing with plants, set in the midst of which is a single wickerwork chair. The courtyard is in shade this early in the day, with the sunlight only reaching some of the highest leaves, but Spiros can see what a perfect place it must be to sit when the sun is higher in the sky. He opens the door and the air in the enclosed space smells of earth and ozone, as if it has just rained.

The cat meows again and he leaves his observations and searches the cupboards until he finds the cat food. He cleans the bowl and fills it again, and tops up the water, and watches the cat eat ravenously. He crouches, stroking the animal, which raises its hindquarters in response.

'There, you are happier now,' Spiros says, and he rocks back on his heels and just watches.

When the cat finishes it asks for more and Spiros does not hesitate. He watches it eat half of this second helping too before he makes his way back out to the shop and into the cool morning air.

Cosmo is coming out of his gate, opposite, with his bag over his shoulder as Spiros leaves the shop, and for a moment Spiros panics, trying to gauge whether he can sneak back inside before he is spotted.

Too late – Cosmo turns and sees him, letting out a surprised 'Oh!'

'Er, I'm …' Spiros feels tongue-tied with guilt.

'Oh,' Cosmo exclaims again, 'I didn't mean for you to feed the cat this morning as well.'

He holds out his hand, smiling cheerfully, and for a moment Spiros is confused, until he realises Cosmo is asking for the key.

'But thank you, Spiro, you've saved me a job. You are a good man,' he says, and he kicks down the stand of his motorbike, flings his leg over the saddle and revs the bike into life. With a smile and a wave, he drives away.

Spiros exhales noisily, surprised to find he has been holding his breath.

'What on earth are you doing here?' the voice of an unseen spectator hisses as Cosmo disappears down the road, and Spiros finds himself tensing up all over again. Takis emerges from behind a bush.

'You surprised me!' Spiros exclaims, and then, a little sulkily, he says, 'I was feeding the cat.'

'You mean you snuck into my house and stole the key to feed a bloody cat?' Takis's voice is louder now.

'She was hungry.'

'I got woken at this unearthly hour for that!'

'Why are you here, anyway?' Spiros frowns.

'Someone woke me up coming into my house and stealing from my pockets.'

Takis sounds cross and Spiros is not sure what to do or say, so he hops nervously from one foot to the other and clears his throat.

'It was hungry, and when I fed it, it purred,' he mutters, but he does not really expect Takis to understand.

'Sometimes I despair of you! Are you *trying* to draw attention to us?'

He is clearly waiting for an answer, but Spiros can't think what to say and considers it better to stay quiet.

Takis sighs and his shoulders slump. 'Well,' he says, 'as we are up, we might as well go and look at the boat, think about your dive. Better to see it in the daylight and work out where it is relative to the pier, that sort of thing. Prepare a little, as it were.'

He puts his hands in his pockets and saunters off towards the orange orchards. It looks as if they are going to walk to Saros again, and with the sun beginning to warm the air, and the slightest of breezes, Spiros anticipates the journey with pleasure.

Once through the trees and on the seashore looking out across the blue, he is reminded of the fish beneath the surface, and the prospect of seeing them again tonight generates a little thrill.

'Are there fish in the harbour?' he asks.

'Is the harbour part of the sea?'

Spiros thinks this means 'yes', but he is not sure and he senses that if he asks any more questions Takis will either get angry or tease him.

A seagull follows them, high in the sky, occasionally calling out its lonely cry … Up ahead, a lizard sits sunbathing on a stone in the middle of path; it darts into the undergrowth as their footsteps approach. The bees are busy around the clumps of flowers on the orange trees, and a pair of butterflies orbit one another in an undulating dance through the trees.

Ordinarily Spiros would take delight in the sights and sounds around him, but recent events weigh heavy on his mind. Certainly there have been moments recently that he would not change for the world – the fish, for example, and feeding Poppy's cat this morning, listening to it purr and feeling the softness of its fur. But there are other things that he would quite happily forget if he could. 'Borrowing' Mitsos's truck and Poppy's diving suit, sneaking about in the shadows round the boat – these do not sit well with him, and the thought of them shortens his breath, and his eye starts twitching.

'You know, with your lungs you could be a sponge diver,' Takis announces suddenly. 'I had an uncle who was a sponge diver. He went to Kalymnos as a teenager and never came back. If there were sponges in the sea round here you would have a job for life.'

Spiros manages a half smile but the picture that emerges from Takis's words is all too familiar. He would dive, and Takis would sit on the shore, selling the sponges to the foreign girls. Most of the money would stay in Takis's pocket, apart from a little that Takis would let him have to cover his essentials. If he wanted money for something special – a plant for his mama, for example, or a candle to light in the church on Sundays – he would have to ask Takis for it, and that always feels like a fight, like he has to justify himself. He mentioned this to his mama once, hoping for her advice, but she had scowled and muttered something about Takis being no good and said he should find other friends, which surprised him. He has learnt now not to talk to Mama about Takis and keeps his own counsel on this subject. He glances sideways at his friend and they walk on in silence.

Saros town looms in the distance as they draw near; the orange groves give way to squat cottages, and then two-storey houses and stark concrete apartment blocks. The harbour is in the oldest part of town, with grand Venetian mansions crowded around the main square, facing each other across roads too narrow for a car to pass. Spiros looks up at these as they go by, takes in the decoration under the eaves and around the windows, appreciates the balanced proportions. Swathes of shocking bougainvillea trail across the streets above head height, draped from one balcony to another.

A flotilla of shiny yachts are tied up to the harbour wall, lined up in a neat row with Dutch and German flags flying from the crosstrees. Their pristine appearance makes George's boat seem even sadder in comparison. The tourists lounge on deck, chatting, drinking beer. One or two have gathered at the quayside and are peering down into the water at George's boat, pointing, talking loudly. One laughs, and the others join in. Takis scowls.

George's boat wavers in its coat of blue and Takis stands a little apart from the group of foreigners, stares down at it, rubbing his chin.

'Okay,' he says quietly, 'here's what I think. I think, judging by its position, it pretty much went straight down, so it makes sense that not all the air would have been able to escape when it sank. I reckon you'll find pockets of air, maybe in the saloon, at roof level, most likely in the toilets.'

Spiros tries to understand why the toilets would have air in them, and it takes him a minute to realise that Takis means that the air will be trapped at the tops of the rooms, and not actually in the toilets! He nods his head vigorously.

'So, if there is air, then you can stay down there until you have found the gold.' Takis rubs his hands together. 'Just think, tomorrow morning we will be maybe thousands of euros richer, in solid gold, my friend. Imagine that!'

At the mention of riches, Spiros has visions of sitting in cafés all day long, drinking as many milkshakes as he likes, but the thought of swimming with the fish is more immediate. 'Will the fish be able to get inside the boat?' he asks.

Takis gives him sharp look. 'Depends on whether the hatch is open.' He looks back down. 'Did we lock it after we …' He leans closer and whispers, 'You know what.'

'You mean sank the boat?' Spiros asks.

'Shhh!' Takis hisses. 'You are never to say those words again, do you understand me?'

Spiros's eye begins to twitch and he looks down into the water at the black square where the hatch must be, whether open or closed. Surely it wouldn't be black if it was closed?

They spend the rest of the day wandering around Saros. Around lunchtime they are invited for coffee by an acquaintance of Takis's, who is sitting by himself with a frappe. Takis makes small talk but avoids any mention of George or the boat.

By late afternoon, the heat becomes oppressive and they find a bench under a tree, where Takis falls asleep, his head lolling backwards, mouth open. Spiros watches a group of tiny brown birds that hop around the pavement in front of the bench. A man walks past eating a sandwich and they scatter briefly, returning as soon as he is gone to fight over the trail of crumbs he has left behind him. A stray dog comes sniffing, begging for food, but as Spiros has none to give it, it settles for a pat on the head and lies down at his feet and falls asleep. Spiros settles himself on the bench too, intending to rest for just a moment, and wakes some time later with the dappled sunshine caressing his face through the leaves.

The evening sees them wandering around town again. Takis spends half an hour or so browsing the ropes and shackles and other nautical items in the chandler's. Outside, they bump into Mitsos, who has come into town for charcoal from the shop next door. Takis chats away about this and that, but Spiros finds it hard to meet his eye, remembering how they took his truck without his permission.

Eventually Mitsos says he must go, and Takis leads them on a tour of the bars, loitering outside each for half an hour or so, no doubt hoping someone will come along whom he knows and invite them in for a drink. It doesn't happen, and the evening draws into night, the town grows quiet and a full moon rises.

'I suppose we can start to think about you going diving,' Takis says as they near the harbour for what must be the tenth time that day.

Spiros feels like he has spent the day walking in circles around the town, and if it were not for the promise of seeing the fish he would certainly go home to bed. Before they actually reach the harbour, Takis swerves off towards the bushes that grow outside the chandler's shop, and Spiros's eye twitches and his heart beats in his ears when he sees Takis plunge a hand into one of the bushes and pull out what might be the biggest torch he has ever seen and a pair of diving goggles.

'You … stole … them?' he stammers, not believing his eyes.

'Borrowed. We'll take them back tomorrow.' Takis is blasé. 'It's waterproof,' he adds, as if this makes the theft all right.

'But we don't even know the chandler.' Spiros's mouth is dry.

'Like I said, he'll never know. And besides, when we find the gold we can buy him ten new ones if he wants. Twenty, even!' Takis marches off towards the harbour, leaving Spiros to follow in his wake.

'I'll keep an eye out for the port police,' Takis says. 'The port police keep a man on watch all night, in a prefabricated cabin on the quayside, but by this time he will be watching television or playing cards with a friend. The cabin is too far away for it to be likely that the sound of you climbing into the water will attract attention' – but he looks nervously down the pier, at the glow that emanates from the windows.

'They're a lazy bunch,' Takis reassures himself, 'and there's no reason for them to come outside unless we make a noise. Right, might be an idea to take your shoes and socks off, maybe your shirt too.'

Spiros has come prepared and he strips down to a pair of baggy shorts.

'Here.' Takis thrusts the torch in his hands. Its face is as wide as his hand span. He will be able to see all sorts of fish with this.

'So, where am I looking?' he asks, trying to focus his mind on the purpose of the dive.

'Everywhere. We don't know where George hid the gold, so open up all the cupboards and compartments. Go!'

Takis hands him the goggles and pushes him towards the steps, which provide a quiet seat on Sundays for the fishermen, who dangle their legs and trail their lines into the harbour. The sea looks impenetrable in the dark, with the moon reflecting off the surface, turning the water into oil. But when Spiros tests the brine with his toes it feels warmer than he expected, and the surface ripples, luring him in. The darkness makes him hesitate but he remembers the night before, how the torch lit up the shoals of fish, reflecting off their scales. Tonight he has a bigger torch, and he will concentrate on spotting the fish if he gets scared.

With a last look up at Takis, he switches the torch on, takes a deep breath and slips under the surface, heading down towards George's boat.

Chapter 4

The new torch is very bright, and it seems to attract the fish, and to Spiros's delight a large shoal swims past moments after he enters the water. They drift slowly, lazily, and then suddenly dart away in perfect unison, as if guided by some unseen force. There are many more fish than there were last night by the jetty in the village, and Spiros soon forgets what he is supposed to be diving for, and he spends his first lungful of air watching the different marine creatures come and go.

There seems to be endless variety – some with long, finger-like tails, others with long frilly ones and fins that make him think of mermaids. A school of tiny black-and-shimmering-white fish flash past, followed by a slow, fat group that are deep blue purply-grey, and yet more striped orange and green. It is a wonderland, and he would stay underwater all night if he could, but he must breathe, and reluctantly he breaks the surface for air.

'Is the hatch open?' Takis hisses, reminding him what he is supposed to be doing. Without answering, Spiros takes another deep breath and once more dives beneath the surface.

It is hard to ignore the fish and not pause to watch them on his second dive, but he kicks with his legs and heads down into the depths, lighting up the way with the torch. To his delight, a large stripy fish leads the way, and he follows it through the hatch, which is open after all.

Spiros has not thought about what the interior of the boat will look like underwater, but even if he had he would not have been prepared for the chaos that greets him. The floorboards have been lifted by the water and float near the level of the roof. The cushions on the saloon seats have lifted too, but they are waterlogged and hang, swollen, halfway up. Below them, the lids on the lockers beneath the seats flap loosely on their hinges, like the shells of giant clams. Glass jars full of screws have floated up out of these lockers, along with plastic storage containers, and a toolbox that presumably still has air trapped inside it. There's a roll of some kind of tape that has been partially unfurled by the current and hangs in the water, waving this way and that as if it were alive. Several waterlogged books line the floor, along with various tubes and hoses, and a stack of maps – George's nautical charts, presumably – which slowly flap as if preparing to swim away. They must have floated out of the chart table and unfurled with the currents. Many smaller items – cigarette lighters, pencils, a digital camera, things he would have expected to sink – float around in the mix … A number of fish swim lazily amongst the debris, flicking their fins and nibbling at the cushions. As Takis predicted, there is air trapped inside the boat, and large bubbles roll around the ceiling, above the floorboards. With all the debris, it's hard to reach them, and Spiros will need more air soon.

He wriggles round to face the toilet door and opens it with caution. There isn't much mess in here: some disposable razor blades, an aerosol can, a plastic nail brush. But more importantly there is a large bubble of air trapped in the small space, into which Spiros pokes his face with relief, taking a deep breath. He turns back and grabs the edges of the doorframe, using them to pull himself back into the saloon, and begins his search.

He tries to work quickly but methodically, making a search of each of the lockers under the seats, pulling out spanners, engine spares and all sorts of other items that he cannot identify. He doesn't really know what he is looking for. A small box, perhaps, which will be heavy – he knows that gold is heavy. He works his way along one line of lockers, holding the torch in one hand and grabbing at the edge of the seats with the other, fighting the buoyancy that tries to lift him to the surface. It soon becomes clear that this is a hopeless task. There are so many lockers, so many spaces under the floors where a small box could be hidden. It would be hard enough to find it in the daylight, if the yacht were floating. But here, in the dark, underwater! It seems impossible. But Takis will not be happy if he comes up too soon, and he may just get lucky and find what they are looking for. His lungs are protesting, though – he must get more air. The air pocket is smaller on his return, having been emptied of one lungful of air, and it is difficult to guess how many more times he can rely on what is there.

He checks the second toilet, and sure enough there is another air pocket there. This gives him confidence and he continues to search the saloon and the two rear cabins, lifting the plywood covers reluctantly off the bunks to search the spaces underneath. George has used every available space for storage, and there is some order to the way he has arranged things. Spiros finds a plastic bag full of ancient mobile phones under one of the bunks, and another with power supplies. There are endless spares for the engine, a roll of fibreglass matting, a stack of life jackets that fight for their freedom only to be halted by the cabin roof. George's clothes are bloated, expanded with the water they have soaked up, in a locker.

The more Spiros searches, the greater the mess inside the boat from the quantity of items he has removed from the lockers and storage spaces. It's tiring, too, trying to hold the torch in one hand whilst searching with the other, and all the time kicking his feet to stay down, all the time fighting against the buoyancy that wants to send him to the surface. Spiros is not managing to hold his breath for as long as he could at the start, and the time he needs to rest between dives is increasing. His precious store of air is getting used up, and he won't be able to stay down much longer.

On his next dive, he opens the cupboard under the sink, grabs at the pots and pans that are stacked in there, and almost jumps out of his skin when a rubbery greyish mass shoots out after them and attaches itself to his arm. In his panic he loses half his air in a silent scream before he realises it is a harmless octopus, and he laughs in relief as his heart rate slowly subsides to its normal levels. The creature seems happy on his arm, wrapping its tentacles around him, exploring the surface of his skin. It seems to flow from one spot to another, as if it is made out of some fluid substance, and Spiros is fascinated. Moving slowly, he makes his way back to the bathroom, where he takes a fresh gulp of air, careful not to dislodge the animal. He examines it closely, watching as the colour of its skin changes subtly to match his arm. Then, just as suddenly as it attached itself to him, the octopus unwraps its tentacles from around his limb and shoots off at a great speed, streamlined like a rocket. Spiros watches it go, a big grin fixed to his face. Never mind the gold – this dive was worth it just for those magical few moments with the octopus! Not that Takis will understand, but either way, his air is almost all used up and he is exhausted. It's time to go.

After taking a last deep breath, he ducks under the surface again and heads for the steps and the hatch that leads out of the boat and up towards the surface. Some of the floorboards have collected around the hatch opening and Spiros has to push these out of the way in order to get through. There's a shiny black briefcase there too, and it reminds him of George for some reason. It seems terribly sad that George's domain has been reduced to this watery mess, and he has a desire to salvage something of it, to take a reminder of the old captain with him. And so, grasping the handle of the briefcase, and after one last look around the interior of the boat, he kicks his legs strongly, heads up through the hatch and towards the surface.

As his head breaks the surface of the water and he gulps deep breaths of fresh air, he feels a slight sense of sadness over the loss of his private watery world. It was magical down there, with the fish, and with the feeling that George was somehow there with him. It was a place where he was in control, capable, self-sufficient, doing something that it turns out he is really rather good at. Something Takis cannot do.

'Oh, thank God and all who are merciful.' Takis grips him by the forearm and pulls at him, lifting him some way out of the water. 'I thought you had drowned!' He seems genuinely concerned. 'You okay?'

Spiros takes more deep breaths, and grins widely.

'I saw an octopus!' he announces.

'And the gold?' Takis asks.

'It changed colour! And it crawled up my arm ...'

'You did look for the gold?' Takis demands.

Spiros tries to put the memory of the fish and the octopus out of his mind.

'It was such a mess down there. Everything was floating about, and I couldn't see into all the cupboards ...'

Will Takis be angry that he didn't manage to find the gold? How can he explain how difficult it was down there?

'I did bring this,' he offers, holding up the briefcase,

'It is heavy?'

'Not really.'

Takis takes the briefcase anyway and pops open the catches. The water drains out, leaving a pile of soggy paperwork and a notebook, sealed in a ziplock bag. Takis pokes at the papers, shrugs and snaps the lid closed again. He sits heavily by the steps and runs his fingers through his thinning hair.

Spiros starts to put his clothes back on.

Chapter 5

By the time they are back in the village Spiros is mostly dry, although his shorts have left an uncomfortable wet patch in the seat of his trousers.

'And you are sure you looked everywhere?' Takis asks for the hundredth time.

'I looked in every locker I could get to, and I took up the boards in the bottoms of the lockers and looked in the spaces under there.'

'But Babis seemed so sure,' Takis muses. 'What about the kitchen? Did you look in the cutlery drawer? Where he kept the plates and the pans?'

Spiros thinks again of the octopus.

'I looked! But I didn't really know what I was looking for, did I? I mean, they could have been in a box, or a bag, anything …'

This seems to make no impact on Takis, who presses on in the same vein.

'Is there anywhere else you could have gone? I mean, if we unscrewed the legs of the table and removed that, or took out the engine?'

Spiros had avoided looking too closely around the engine. The blackness of it frightened him, and to put his hands anywhere near it felt like he would risk losing his fingers. But he is not going to tell Takis this. He swallows nervously and half chokes, doubling over in a fit of coughing. Will Takis know he is not telling the whole truth? He rubs his eye before it starts to twitch.

But Takis gives him a slap on the back and carries on walking.

'Well, I suppose you could dive again,' he says. 'Although there doesn't seem much point if you are sure.' He sounds downhearted.

Spiros swings George's briefcase as they walk. It's the sort of case you might find in the hand of a bank manager, or someone else in a position of authority, in a shiny office in Saros. This thought adds a little bounce to his step.

'Right, I'm going to see Babis. If he's given us the runaround I'll …'

The implication is clear. When Takis says *he* is going to see Babis, what he really means is 'we'. But Spiros's trousers are still wet and he really needs to change them, and he doesn't much want to see the lawyer anyway. He swings the briefcase, which arches forward, its weight pulling him on a step. Back it goes, slowing the next step. Takis's unpredictable moods feel like that, urging him forward and holding him back, keeping him off balance.

As he swings the case, it occurs to him that he does not have to go with Takis, if he chooses to do otherwise.

He will not go with Takis.

He will go home, change his shorts and see if his mama is all right, and maybe look through the contents of the briefcase by himself.

'Come on, then,' Takis says as they reach Babis's door.

'I'm going home.'

Takis's eyes widen suddenly, and the whites show on all sides.

'Oh.' He falters and his feet shuffle, as if he cannot decide which way to go without Spiros at his side.

But Spiros has made his mind up and he turns in the direction of home, swinging the briefcase forward.

His mama's door is closed, and she could be sleeping, so he enters his own rooms and puts the briefcase on the kitchen table. The case is made of black plastic textured to look like leather, with a smooth plastic handle and shiny metal clasps. Spiros puts a thumb on each clasp and snaps them open simultaneously, just like they do in the movies when a ransom is given. The lid springs up and the smell of the sea is released. The papers inside are a soggy mess, the pages stuck together, and he lifts them out as a lump and puts them on the doorstep in the sun. The top sheet has the words *Crew List* printed at the top, and a series of lines printed below this. The lines are smeared blue, as if the form has been filled in with pen and the water has smudged the writing. There is a hardback blue notebook, too, but its pages are stuck together, and when Spiros prises it open the pages tear. They are also smudged with blue, and he puts it on the doorstep with the rest of the papers. Apart from the papers and the blue notebook, there is an old train ticket, a strip of photographs of women with blonde hair, a comb with half the teeth missing, a fifty-drachma coin and a book of postage stamps. These all join the papers on the doorstep, and Spiros turns his attention to the last item – the ziplock plastic bag.

He opens this carefully, sliding the plastic zip, to find that the notebook inside is perfectly dry. He lifts it out carefully and, resting it on the table, opens the cardboard cover.

Aida 1941, he reads on the first page. He looks back at the cover for a clue. Maybe it is not George's after all. He opens it again and turns another page.

There is a date and then …

Maraveyas – 200l water, 50l diesel.

Paid €150. Total €300.

Well, that must be George. Spiros turns to another page, at random: *Tracy came past today*. Below the text is a drawing of a boat, the line of the keel drawn over many times to get the curve right. Spiros doesn't know anyone named Tracy. But perhaps Tracy is the name of another boat? His cheeks burn hot; either way, it feels like he is prying. George may be dead but does that make it all right to read his personal notes? He flips the book open to another page anyway.

Coffee with Takis and Spiros.

He sits up a bit taller and puts a finger under the words, reading carefully.

Takis is not kind to Spiros. He is a bully.

A fish is drawn below this, bubbles rising from its mouth that circle the words.

'George thinks Takis bullies me?' Spiros's lips move, sounding these words in a whisper.

He looks up from the book and out of the door. Surely Takis is his friend, even if he can be rather grumpy sometimes? And yet George thought of him as a bully; he thought this to such a degree that he wrote it in this book, which was special enough to wrap in a plastic bag. His eye starts to twitch. Is he? Is Takis a bully? George's words sort of fit, and the fact that they do is disturbing. Takis is only looking out for him. Isn't he? His breathing grows shallow.

He turns the page, but the next entry is longer and nothing to do with him or Takis.

Picked up a group of tourists from the jetty, two German families, ten people in all. Stella arranged it, and asked me to leave some flyers for her guests etc.

Must remember to fill in a crew list and register the charter with the port police.

And then another entry on the next page:

Coffee with Commander Demosthenes today. He asked after business and I remembered I still haven't declared the charters from Stella's. Is there any point now? I might even get a fine if I declare them too late.

Perhaps better to keep quiet and make sure I declare them in the future. But for now, at least there's a little cash in hand.

Picked another group up off the jetty in the village, four Dutch, four English and two French. I forgot to ask for their passport numbers so I cannot declare them to the port police. The cash in hand is very useful, no bookkeeping and no tax. But tomorrow I will make a crew list, do it correctly from now on.

Spiros turns the page.

I couldn't bring myself to write out a crew list today. The group arrived late, I thought they weren't coming, so I deemed it

*better to push off than get involved in paperwork. I am
beginning to think that this is a better way to work. It cuts down
so much of the headache of paperwork and making special trips
to the port police office to register the daily crew. If the
authorities made it easier I would do it, but as it is I have paid so
much tax over the years I feel I have a right to a little black
money.*

After this is a cartoon of a cat's face with a grin that
reaches from ear to ear.

He reads on:

*The port police commander called me over when I saw him
having coffee this morning. He wanted to know where I was
going with an empty boat every morning. I wonder if he
suspects, I will have to be smarter …*

*Took a couple of tourists from Saros town today as a cover
for the rest of the week, which is booked solid from Stella's. I
must fill out a crew list at least once a week or the port police
may grow suspicious enough to investigate. I am glad Stella is
ignorant of how the process should be. I would hate to implicate
her.*

Spiros turns the page. There are many more entries
listing the number of people George picked up from the
jetty in the village. If he did not file crew lists for these
trips, there will be no record of his earnings. Which means,
if the book is to be believed, that he was making a fortune,
or at least more than the accountant was aware of! Adding
up the actual figures listed feels beyond him, but he gets
the impression that George was earning hundreds of euros
some days.

Spiros closes his eyes and tries to think. Something
is lurking in his brain, something about George making a
lot of money. He never looked like he had much money at

44

all, so where did it go? Was he buying gold with it? Of course! – doesn't this virtually prove that there is gold on the boat?

His instinct is to run next door and tell Takis what he has discovered, but then what does he have to tell him, exactly? Not much! He turns another page, absorbed in the drawings now. He can only read so much before his eyes hurt and his head throbs, but the pictures are great. There is a mermaid and a seahorse, a man on a bicycle and a drawing of the little kitchen stove on the boat, and the sink next to it. Under this drawing are the words *Seek and you shall find*.

Spiros shuts the book and puts it back in the plastic bag. He enjoys resealing the top with the plastic zip, which he does with clumsy fingers, then he squeezes it against his chest to get the air out and places it back in the briefcase.

'Seek and you shall find,' he mutters.

A shadow fills the doorway – Takis.

'What did you say?' Takis demands.

'Oh, just something I read in George's book,' Spiros tells him. 'Seek and you shall find.' Maybe he should have stayed silent, but he is not sure why.

'Really?' Takis sounds interested. 'Was there anything more?' He comes in uninvited and picks up the book, turning it in his hands in its plastic cover.

'No.' Spiros rests his head on his hand to stop the twitching. It was not he who called Takis a bully, and he has no need to feel guilty. 'Just lots of drawings.'

'Of what?'

'Lots of things. A mermaid, some fish, the little stove and the sink next to it. The cupboard below.'

Takis takes the book out of its plastic case and flicks through the drawings. He stops when he comes to the one of the stove and the sink with the words underneath.

'Babis said the notes specifically say there is gold on board. He says he feels that it must still be there as the last note was dated just two days before he died. We've missed the gold. I suggest …'

He looks carefully at the drawing. The way George has drawn it, the door of the cupboard is open and inside the shelf is bare.

'What do you think these dots mean?' He points inside the cupboard where there are dots marked carefully, one at each corner.

'Maybe they are nails or screws, for detail, to make it look real?' Spiros offers. That's what he would do if he could draw, put in details like that.

'Did you look in the cupboard?'

'Yes, and I took out the pans that were in there, but there was nothing else.'

'Did you see these screws?'

'I didn't notice.'

'Perhaps we should dive again.' It is not a question and Spiros wonders why Takis has used the word 'we' when he clearly means 'you'. He does it all the time, and Spiros starts to feel angry about it, but then the octopus comes to his mind again. A vision forms – a dream, really

– in which he is feeding the octopus. It is sitting on his hand again, eating, and it is his friend.

'What do octopuses eat?' he asks.

Takis gives him a withering look and shakes his head.

'So it's settled. We'll dive again, take a look inside this cupboard, look for new screws. Take a screwdriver with you.'

It is nearly evening when they arrive, strolling past the eucalyptus just before the harbour once again. Spiros swings the plastic bag he is carrying, with the mask and the torch in it. This time he has brought a towel, too, and a change of shorts, so he doesn't have to walk home in wet trousers again. High up in the branches of the eucalyptus tree, hidden amongst the leaves, an owl calls out, and he stops to look for it.

Takis, on the other hand, cries out, 'What in Saint Christopher!' and starts running.

Spiros turns to watch him, and in the glint of the setting sun he sees a fleet of new, shiny yachts pulling into the harbour.

Spiros scans one boat, then the next, but he sees nothing wrong. He can see no reason for Takis's outburst, or for his wild and uncharacteristic burst of speed in the direction of the pier. Takis stops on the quayside at the spot where George's boat sank under the water, waving his hands frantically, and shouting in the direction of one of the yachts, which is heading straight for him, and which will surely collide with George's boat if it continues on its course. Spiros starts to run too now, waving his arms. The young woman at the bows, with the controller with its big red button in one hand, looks up and smiles and waves back.

'*Stamata!*' Spiros shouts, and a part of his brain, somewhere at the back, wonders if he knows the word in English. The woman is dressed in just a bikini and has long blonde hair. She waves again.

'Stop!' Spiros shouts.

Spiros is on the pier now, next to Takis. But Takis is no longer shouting, or waving his hands. Instead he is scratching his head and looking down into the water. He seems puzzled. Spiros slows to a halt by his side and looks into the water too.

Something seems wrong, and it takes his brain just a moment to register what it is: it is gone!

George's boat, their yacht, is no longer there!

'What? *How?* Taki – where's the boat?' his words stumble out.

But Takis does not answer. His brows lower and he stamps purposefully off up the quayside, leaving Spiros trotting along behind to keep up. Takis appears to be heading towards the port police cabin.

'Are you going to report it stolen?' Spiros asks breathlessly.

Takis raps his knuckles on the plastic door of the cabin and pushes it open forcefully, without waiting for a reply.

'Where's my boat?' he demands as he steps through the door.

Spiros recognises the duty port police man sitting behind the desk inside the cabin but he doesn't know his name. He is a young man, just a boy, really, with a neatly cropped haircut and a smart dark-blue uniform. Despite his youth, he regards Takis coolly, seemingly unfazed by his outburst. 'Good evening, Kyrie Taki,' he replies formally, 'how are you today?'

'I said where's my boat?'

'It was a danger.' He looks out of the window. 'The safety of the harbour is of paramount importance. We did tell you.'

'Told me what? Where's my boat?'

The port police man leans back in his chair and regards Takis for a moment before he replies.

'We lifted it and' – he starts to shuffle through the papers on his desk until he finds the envelope he is looking for – 'here's the bill.' He picks up a pen and looks down at the other papers on his desk.

Takis grabs the envelope, tears it open and roughly unfolds the paper that is within.

'Did you just make this number up!' he demands. 'And why on earth did you bring a crane from Athens? There is a man here …'

'We used the resources approved by the port police – that is how things are done. You were given an opportunity to remove the obstruction yourself, but … Anyway, that is in the past. Now the boat has been impounded, and you will be allowed access to her once the bill for her recovery is settled.' The officer, in his smart uniform, seems to be enjoying the exchange, taking some pleasure in being able to exercise his authority.

'You cannot do this!'

The officer raises an eyebrow and with the pen in his hand taps the bill Takis is holding.

'This is robbery! You cannot stop us from boarding our own vessel.'

'It is not in my control. The vessel has been impounded until we recover what was paid to lift her. That is the law.'

Takis looks again at the bill. Spiros looks over his shoulder. There are a lot of noughts on the end of the number at the bottom of the page.

'I can't pay this.'

The man shrugs. 'Then the boat will remain impounded. But be aware that penalties will accrue. It is better if you settle the debt sooner rather than later.' The man smirks, although there is also an air of boredom in his voice, and his pen taps impatiently on his desk.

'Where is the pound?' Takis says, and Spiros's mouth goes dry.

'It doesn't matter, does it, Kyrie Taki, not unless we have the money that is owed.'

'Now, you listen to me, young man!' Takis snaps at him. 'Where is my boat?'

The port police man seems a little taken aback by the force of Takis's questioning, and he looks up, stops tapping his pen. There is a pause, and finally he says, 'In the yard where the fishermen take their boats out, down along the water's edge.'

He vaguely points along the coast in the direction of the village.

'Past the village?'

The policeman's eyes narrow; he returns Takis's stare but he does not answer.

'Where?' Takis bellows, and Spiros steps back in alarm.

The port police man looks suddenly too young to be here, wearing his smart uniform, and his face flushes white.

'Yes, beyond the village,' he stammers, but he recovers himself quickly. 'Not that it makes any difference to you,' he adds. 'It is fenced, and you cannot get in.'

But he is clearly nervous now, and no longer enjoying the exchange. Spiros feels nervous too, and he edges towards the door, grateful that, for once at least, he is not on the receiving end of Takis's anger. He feels for the boy, though, who now seems very young – just out of school probably, with barely the shadow of a moustache on his top lip.

As Spiros turns abruptly and stamps towards the door of the cabin, Spiros and the boy make eye contact and an understanding passes between them. It lasts only a second, and then Spiros turns too and hurries after Takis.

Chapter 6

'I'll bet the yacht's being held up at the yard in the marshland beyond the village,' Takis says as he heads past the eucalyptus tree and along the path. 'You know the one, where the fishermen all take their boats out of the water.'

'I wonder if the octopus managed to get out?' Spiros asks, but Takis is several paces ahead, looking at his feet, deep in thought.

'I've only been round to that yard once or twice, but I know there are several keys knocking about. I should think every fisherman in the village has one,' Takis ponders aloud.

'If they brought the boat up quickly, the octopus might not have had time to get out. He might have hidden somewhere.' This thought makes Spiros sad.

'I can't really remember how secure it was, but there's definitely a fence of some sort around it. And I'm pretty sure I remember a kennel, so maybe there are dogs.'

'A dog wouldn't eat an octopus, would it?' Spiros's voice cracks as he speaks, it is an alarming thought.

'What? What are you talking about? Oh, I see, keep the dog occupied with something tasty while we sneak in. We might be better off with chicken scraps from Stella's eatery.'

'No!' A horrible image of an octopus frightened by a dog fills Spiros's mind.

'Why not? Dogs love chicken.'

Spiros frowns, struggling to follow the thread of the conversation, hoping Takis will say more so he can catch up without admitting that he doesn't know what is being said.

The beach curves around a corner and the edge of the village jetty comes into sight.

'There.' Takis stops to point. 'If you look way past the jetty, beyond that bunch of eucalyptus trees, you see where there is a dark patch that is all thickets and undergrowth. In there is where the boatyard is.'

Spiros peers into the distance. It's a long way away and he is already tired.

'We could keep walking, go check it out – or we could rest up awhile and go at sunset, and then if it is the right place we can use the cover of night to go in.'

It almost sounds like a question but Spiros knows Takis better than that, and he also knows that 'we can go in' really means *he* can go in. He opens his mouth to say something, but then wonders again about the octopus.

'Will the boat still have water in it?' he asks.

Takis looks at him and starts to laugh, but he stops quite suddenly.

'Actually, that's not as stupid as it sounds. It must have a drain hole, right? I mean, there's the hose we disconnected, and if water came in there, it must be able to go out there too.'

Spiros wonders if he should mention that he reattached the hose but decides against it.

'But even if it drains from there,' Takis continues, 'it wasn't the lowest point, so the water will still be up to your ankles, if not higher. I never thought of that. Do you have a pair of rubber boots?'

Spiros is about to say that he is glad there will still be water in the boat, for the octopus, but then decides not to share this thought with Takis. It would be nice if the water was higher than the level of his ankles, and for the boat to be full of fish and octopus and all manner of marine creatures. Imagine that – being able to just jump into the boat to see all that wildlife any time he likes!

He starts to chuckle at the thought, enjoying how silly and upside down the notion of a boat being kept full of water, instead of empty and floating in the water, would sound.

'What are you laughing at?' Takis snaps, but he doesn't wait for an answer. They are nearly at the jetty now, and they turn inland towards the village.

As they approach the village square, Takis speaks again. 'Just think, tomorrow all our hardships will be over,' he says, and he lets out a long heavy breath as he heads towards the kiosk.

'*Yeia sou*, Vasso,' he greets the kiosk owner inside her wooden hut.

She must have had a recent delivery as the wooden shelf around the outside is stacked with boxes of chewing gum, plastic cups in cellophane wrappers that you can fill with water and shake to make an instant cold coffee, and packets of dry-looking crackers. There are tall tubes of crisps stacked on top of each other, packets of wafer biscuits, strips of cardboard from which individual tubes of quick-drying glue can be detached, and endless other things.

'*Yeia sou*, Taki. How are you, Spiro?' Vasso turns away from the packets of cigarettes that she is stacking against the inside walls of her kiosk to face them with a smile.

'Hello, Vasso.' Spiros likes Vasso.

Just by the opening where she takes the money from her customers, she keeps a box of individually wrapped sweets and she will usually insist that he take one, whether he has bought anything or not. Most often, if he is at the kiosk it is because he is with Takis, who is buying cigarettes. She also always asks how he is and speaks very kindly to him, and sometimes she gives him a tube of mints. Yes, he likes Vasso.

'Vasso, I'm expecting to be paid tomorrow,' Takis says. Spiros looks at him sharply. 'So if you wouldn't mind I will have a packet of cigarettes and I'll pay you tomorrow.' He smiles broadly. Spiros looks at his feet. His eye feels like it might begin to twitch.

'Ah, payday tomorrow, is it, Taki? Do be sure to come by tomorrow then, and I'll let you have as many packets as you can afford,' Vasso says with a smile.

This makes Spiros smile. He understands this sort of humour, and she winks at him, which makes him feel included.

'Come, Vasso, I've been a loyal customer here for as many years as I can remember. A day wouldn't hurt.'

55

'As you say, a day won't hurt, so I'll see you tomorrow then,' Vasso replies, and she takes a wrapped sweet from her box and offers it to Takis.

Takis scowls and waves the gift away, turns abruptly and marches off in the direction of his house. Spiros is about to follow when Vasso calls him back quietly.

'Hey, Spiro, these are for you.' She hands him a packet of his favourite mints.

'But I ...' he begins, but Vasso pats his hand to silence him and then turns back to her work. He slips the mints in his pocket. He will save them till later when he will sit on his doorstep and suck on them listening to the dull clonk of goat bells and the bleating of the goats as they return to the village, and the cockerel getting the time wrong, and the dogs giving their evening serenade. He will enjoy that. Maybe the owl will be back too. He hasn't heard the owl for a few days.

Takis is waiting by his front door, still scowling.

'I'm going to have a snooze, and you should too. We'll go after dark.'

All images of the pleasant sunset and the sounds of the goats and the dogs fade, and his inner voice says 'that bloody gold', and immediately his face flushes hot at the swear word. But Takis has already headed into his house, and so Spiros is spared having to explain himself. Maybe he should get some sleep if they are to be up all night again.

In his dream, a man is chasing an octopus with a harpoon. Spiros has magic lungs that allow him to breathe

56

underwater and he is swimming fast to save the octopus. The octopus looks scared and as the harpoon is released Spiros puts out his arm and the point of the harpoon bounces off his rock-hard bicep. Another harpoon dart hits him, and then another, and his eyes flutter open as he realises the sensation is real.

'Wake up!' Takis hisses, and he pokes him in the arm once more.

'Ow, that hurts!' Spiros rubs at his bicep.

'Well, get up, we've got work to do,' Takis says. 'Where are your rubber boots?'

'Rubber what?'

Spiros cannot shake his dream off. He needs to save the octopus from Takis's pointy finger. He blinks again and shakes away fantasy from truth.

'Oh yes, boots. Behind the front door.'

'Right, come on.' Takis seems excited and agitated all at once, and eager to be away.

Pulling on his boots over his bare feet, Spiros wonders if he has time to find socks, but Takis is hurrying him.

The moon is out, and sure enough the owl is back, and it hoots at the sight of them.

'Come on, stop dawdling,' Takis urges him, and the two of them set off down the lane, across the deserted square and out the other side to the lane that leads through the orange groves to the seashore.

'Can't we go by road?' Spiros asks. It is dark under the trees.

57

'And risk being seen?'

Takis is in the lead. Spiros stays close as they make their way through the trees and is rewarded by the moon reflected on the sea. It is a beautiful sight and he stops to take it in.

'Oh, do come on,' Takis hisses.

Their route takes them past Stella's hotel, and here Takis crouches low and runs on tiptoe past the floodlit entrance. Spiros copies him, but his boots are rubbing the backs of his calves and his feet slide about in them. They do not fit well at all.

The shoreline beyond the hotel is unfamiliar to him. It is not somewhere he has ventured often, certainly not for any distance. As a boy, his mama forbade it, saying the ground was soft, the marshes dangerous.

'Are you sure this is safe?' he hisses to Takis's back.

Takis switches on his torch, lighting up the path a few metres in front of them. Spiros is happier now there is some light, and he follows close behind Takis. They seem to continue like this for ages, his boots rubbing, feet sliding. The waterline is increasingly strewn with debris as they leave the hotel behind them, and the light shows up interesting things: a red plastic bucket in the shape of a castle, the sole of a shoe. It would be interesting to come this way in the daytime, to see what other treasures there might be. Then the way narrows and the scrubland almost meets the sea, and rocks take over from the sand.

'There's a path through here.' Takis leads the way inland, down a path that cuts between the bushes, and Spiros follows more closely. Nothing is familiar and everything is dark. The moon does its best, but rather than lighting the way it creates shadows that seem to move and fade, then grow dark again.

'I don't like this,' Spiros whispers, frightened that if he speaks too loudly the unseen things in the bushes may come out.

'It widens here.' Takis urges him on without pausing.

The path joins a dirt track just wide enough for a car.

'Taki, how could they have brought the boat this way?' Spiros asks. It seems too rough for any vehicle to pass, let alone a truck with a yacht on the back.

'They didn't. If my memory serves me right, there is a wide road on the other side.'

'Couldn't we have come that way?'

Takis does not answer.

'Right, the yard's just up ahead.' Takis switches the torch off and everything is black for a moment. Neither of them moves as their eyes adjust.

'Here, take this.' Takis hands the torch to Spiros. 'I'll feel the way, you hold onto the back of my shirt.'

Spiros grips Takis's shirt with one hand and holds fast to the torch with the other, and they stumble blindly ahead for a few more steps.

'Well, here's the fence and I see no lights anywhere, so I think we're safe.'

Takis speaks in a normal voice, not whispering, and this alone gives Spiros some confidence. The moon lights up the shapes behind the fence; small fishing boats perch drunkenly on their shallow keels, and bigger ones are supported by wooden crutches, as if they are injured.

'There!' Takis sounds jubilant, and sure enough, there, near the opposite fence, is their yacht.

Spiros clicks on the torch and shines it at the boat.

'Keep the beam low.' Takis pushes the torch down so it shines at the ground. 'I'll check the gate.'

He takes from his pocket a tiny torch no bigger than a pen, which has a very intense beam, and with it he starts to investigate the padlock, but Spiros has spotted something else. On the ground, in the beam of his big torch, is a footprint that is similar to a dog's, but he suspects it is that of a wolf. He shivers with fear but a part of him wants to see more so he follows the track that leads around the other side of the fence.

'Well, this is no use, we'll have to find another way in,' Takis says, and then there is silence.

'Spiro? Spiro, where are you? In the name of all that is holy, where–'

'Here,' Spiros calls, and rapid footsteps tell him Takis is running to join him.

'Can't you stay focused for one minute?' he puffs. 'There I am, trying to find a way in, work out how we'll deal with this, and all you can do is … What *are* you doing, anyway?'

Spiros points.

Takis follows the beam of light.

There, on the ground, the footprints lead up to an area where the wolves, or dogs, or whatever they are, have dug a hole that goes right under the fence.

'I've been finding a way in, too,' Spiros says, and he clenches his teeth, anticipating Takis's anger at his being cheeky; it would not be the first time. Instead, he is surprised to receive a slap on the shoulder.

'Hey, well done! … Right – after you.'

Spiros doesn't need asking twice. He is on his hands and knees and in his heart he is a wolf. Under he goes and out the other side. Takis takes a little longer, and then they stand side by side, Takis with his hands on his hips, admiring the yacht.

The vessel rests on its keel, and thick wooden posts are wedged to stop it from falling over, four or five on each side. Suddenly, from the dark shadows between the boats, comes a growl and the sound of feet padding towards them. Takis moves faster than Spiros could ever have given him credit for and is halfway under the fence before Spiros has even had time to react. Spiros pushes from behind as the growling and patter of feet rushes nearer, and just as he thinks it is all over, there is a yelp and he turns to find the dog half throttling itself on the end of a long chain and snapping at their heels.

Takis is out the other side, and Spiros presses himself up against the fence, his heart pounding. He finds he is sweating, breathing hard, but his panic slowly subsides as he realises the dog can come no closer: its long chain leash will not allow it.

'She can't reach,' Spiros tells Takis.

'It can't right now, but how will we get past it to the boat?' Takis hisses. 'Bloody animal.'

'She's not a …' Spiros is reluctant to say the word. 'She's done nothing wrong. She's just doing her job.'

'It's not allowing us to do ours!'

Takis sounds annoyed. Takis always sounds annoyed these days. Spiros still has the torch in one hand, and he puts the other in his pocket. His fingers play with the tube of mints Vasso gave him earlier. He takes them out and throws one to the dog, which is still growling, although it does not seem so angry, after all. It sniffs nervously and then eats the mint, making strange faces as if the sweet is sticking to his gums. Spiros eats one too and then offers one to Takis.

'Oh, for heaven's sake, get to the boat while it's distracted,' Takis growls in a voice that makes Spiros think of wolves again.

The dog has finished its mint and is now wagging its tail and sitting expectantly.

Spiros holds out another mint and attempts to pat the dog, which responds by wagging its tail and even licks his mint-covered fingers when it has finished its treat.

Takis starts to crawl under the fence again but the dog is immediately back on alert, growling, hackles raised.

'Mangy cur.' Takis backs out and remains on the far side of the fence. 'You'd best go by yourself.'

'As if it would be otherwise,' Spiros mutters to himself, and he eats another mint and pats the dog, which once again wags its tail at him. 'How am I supposed to get up there anyway?'

He looks up at the hulk of the yacht, which towers over him. It seems much bigger than it did when it was in the water.

'Look for a ladder, there's bound to be one.' Takis is now sitting on a rock, as if he expects to have to wait for some time.

With a sigh, Spiros turns on the torch and shines it all around, looking for a ladder. Almost immediately he spots an old olive-picking ladder leaning against a small shack at the back of the enclosure. It is much taller than the half-rotted wooden building and it is heavy. With the handle of the torch in his mouth, he uses both hands and all his balance, slithering in his boots, to manoeuvre it to the boat. It hits the railing with a clang and Takis tuts his disapproval. The dog follows him, tail wagging.

It feels very unsteady as he takes the rungs one at a time, the torch still in his mouth so he can grip tight with both hands.

'Three points of contact.' He recites the words that his mama taught him when he did his first olive pick and which he has said to himself every year since when he is up a tree. It is easier than he expects to get over the railing at the top, but as he lands on the deck the whole boat feels unsteady, as if the wooden posts that are supporting it are not securely positioned.

'Careful!' Takis calls.

The deck is slippery with dew. Inside, the boat is full of water up to perhaps knee level, and the floorboards, the cushions and all the other items have settled in a great heap, with the water reflecting the torchlight back between the gaps in the debris. Spiros climbs down the ladder and pushes his foot between two swollen cushions. The water is deeper than he expected and his boots fill with cold water. As he turns to take another step, the first boot becomes stuck and his foot comes away without it. He shines the torch down to see where the boot is and spots several fish.

'Oh, you poor things.' He immediately starts to search, but not for the gold, or for the boot. Instead, he finds a plastic bag, half floating, with two screwdrivers in it, and he empties them out on the table in the saloon and tries to catch the fish with the bag. There is nowhere really that they can escape to, and he manages to scoop four into his bag and then cannot find any more.

He takes them up on deck, and again he feels the boat rocking slightly with each footstep. Down the ladder, pat the dog, and then over to the fence where Takis is waiting, and under it, clutching his catch. Takis stands, his face expectant.

'Won't be a minute,' Spiros says, and he trots off, as best he can with only one boot, to the water's edge, where he releases his little friends and watches as they swim away.

'What on earth are you doing!' Takis calls.

'Just a second.' He runs back, empty bag in hand.

'What are you up to?' Takis demands.

'Nothing.' Spiros rolls back under the fence. The dog wags its tail in delight and jumps up at him, licking at his face. He takes out the mints, one for himself and one for the dog, and strokes the animal's soft ears. Then he is up the ladder again and onto the deck, and he turns to see Takis standing staring at him, hands on hips, mouth open, before he goes back down below.

The water isn't so cold this time, and as he takes his first step into the saloon he rejoices: the octopus! But as he reaches for his mints and moves a cushion aside he is disappointed – it is only his rubber boot. He pulls it on and tries to remember why he is there.

'Oh yes, the gold.' He is enjoying himself. He still has the image in mind of Takis standing, waiting for him, open-mouthed. It makes him laugh. He eats another mint.

Crouching by the sink, he pushes the floorboards out of the way and looks inside, then stands to retrieve the torch and the screwdrivers, which he left on the table earlier. Sure enough, on the panel at the back of the cupboard there is a screw in each corner, just as they were drawn in the notebook. He puts his hand in his pocket for another mint, only to find it is his last one. Never mind – if the gold is here he can buy many tubes of mints.

He unscrews the panel and pulls it away to reveal an empty triangular space behind it, and the side of the boat, which curves away under the recess.

'Oh,' he says, and he is about to put the panel back when he decides instead to reach a tentative hand down into the space at the back of the cupboard, where he touches something hard.

He grips it and tries to lift it. Whatever it is, it's heavy, and he can slide it left and right so it is definitely not attached. With the torch handle in his mouth once more, he reaches awkwardly in with both hands. There is something else there as well – something small and round in a clear plastic bag. This is easy to pull out and to his absolute delight it looks like a tube of mints. But then George has not only put the mints, if that's what they are, in a plastic bag, but he has also rolled them up in paper and written words down the side. Spiros holds the tube in the torchlight and makes out the letters one by one.

'S-p-i-r-o-s. Hey, that's me! Thanks, George!'

He puts the tube in his pocket, plastic bag and all, and then recalls what he was doing. Once again he reaches with both hands and grips the heavy hidden object, and he lifts with all his strength. It dislodges suddenly, he falls backward, the torch flies from his teeth and he sits with force on one of the brine-soaked cushions. The yacht feels like it rocks with the force of his movements, but he has in his hands a solid metal box that is sealed shut with a strange-looking lock. It is heavy. It must be the gold! He almost wants to yelp with joy but Takis might be cross if he made too much noise.

His trousers, now wet, stick to his legs as he makes his way back out. Both his boots are full of water and make it difficult to climb back down the ladder.

On solid ground again, he pats the dog and puts his hand in his pocket to give it one of George's mints, but Takis is waving at him and so he hurries over to the fence instead and proudly presents the box to his friend.

'The gold?' Takis asks.

'It's locked, but it's heavy, isn't it?' Spiros answers.

Takis takes the box and puts his hand out for the torch.

'Oh! I left it on board.' Spiros sets off for the boat again. He will give the dog another mint – a thank-you mint.

'Leave it!' Takis grabs at his shirt to stop him. 'Come on, let's get back home and crack this beauty open!'

He turns and sets off back the way they came, leaving Spiros to empty his boots. There is a massive blister under one of Spiros's heels and the skin has rubbed off the back of both his calves, but he cannot linger: Takis has gone and he doesn't want to go through the scrubland on his own.

They must have been on the boat for ages, and the walk must have been a long one, because as they enter the village the sun is peeking over the horizon, once again lifting the blanket of night from the terracotta roof tiles.

Takis has put the box under his shirt and he is holding it with both hands. No one is about, not even Vasso, who is the first to open up in the morning, so once they are past the square and in their lane Takis slows his pace.

'I can't wait to open it,' Spiros says, and he puts his hand out to carry the treasure for the last bit of the journey, but Takis is not letting it go.

Chapter 7

'It's some sort of safe.'

Takis sounds like he knows what he is talking about, but Spiros looks for himself anyway. Takis often sounds like he knows what he is talking about, but recently it doesn't always seem to be the case. And was it not he, Spiros, who dived for the gold – twice? Was it not he who found the way under the fence and calmed the dog, and he who actually found the gold!

'Ha!' he says out loud, but he gives no explanation to Takis.

'Let's just smash it,' Takis says, and without warning he throws the metal box down hard on Spiros's kitchen floor.

'Shh, you'll wake Mama!' Spiros exclaims. 'And you'll break the floor.'

He picks up the box, which appears unharmed. There is a chip out of one of the tiles on the kitchen floor, but it is not the only one, and Spiros cannot be sure it was not there all along.

'Have you got a hammer?' Takis asks, taking the box and inspecting it closely.

Spiros has screwed a series of hooks into the wall behind the front door, and he hangs tools, coats, and anything else that he considers useful on these. He has a habit of losing things and this system means that some items, at least, have a place, and he can find them when he needs them. Amongst these is a hammer, which he retrieves for Takis.

Takis kneels with the box in front of him on the floor, raises the hammer with both hands and smashes it down.

'Shhh!' Spiros says again, looking at the wall that divides his mama's room from the rest of the house.

'It's bombproof!' Takis declares.

'Let's take it to Babis, he might know what to do.'

'Good idea.' Takis is on his feet and before Spiros can replace his hammer on its hook he is out of the door.

Barefoot, and hopping because of the blister, Spiros runs to catch Takis up.

'Will he be up yet?' he calls.

'If not, he will be soon!' Takis raps at Babis's door.

It's a few minutes before a bleary-eyed Babis opens the door.

'What the heck …? Oh, great, it's you two. What do you want now? You know the port police have impounded the boat, don't you? I think it's time you …' But he spies the box that Takis is holding out to him and doesn't finish his sentence.

'How do we open it?' Takis asks.

'Come in, come in.' Babis shoves the door to open it further but the coats and jackets have fallen off the hook again and it jams. Takis squeezes his way through and Spiros follows.

'Let me see.' Babis takes the box and turns it around in his hands. 'It's a safe. You won't open this without the key.'

'We need a key?' Takis turns scornful eyes on Spiros as if it is his fault that they have no key.

Spiros doesn't mind if they have to go back – he'll see the dog again and maybe he can have a really good look to make sure the octopus is not trapped, although he doubts it is still there. Either way, he will have to wait till his foot has healed. It hurts so much this morning that he can hardly bear to put any weight on it.

'Not a key, exactly. A code, four numbers. Look, this is the dial.'

Babis sets the box on the kitchen table and points to the front of it, which has four little wheels on it with numbers embossed on them. The lawyer sits heavily and yawns, wrapping his dressing gown more tightly around himself. Takis and Spiros follow suit, and they sit staring at the safe. Spiros listens to the clock ticking on the wall, and then outside he hears the first cockerel crow, followed by another. Some shutters bang open and a distant car changes gear.

'A number, you say?' Takis says.

'Yes, four digits.'

Four digits. Four numbers, like a birthday. A memory stirs in Spiros's mind, but it is just beyond his reach, teasing him.

'Is there no other way to get it open?' Takis asks. He sounds flat, defeated.

Babis shrugs. 'What do *you* think? You can see it's been designed that way.'

Four letters appear in Spiros's mind: *Aida*. Could they have something to do with the box?

'Aida,' he says. Takis looks up at him briefly, then turns back to the box.

'What if we get a drill, or one of those hammer things they use to dig up the road?' he says to Babis.

Babis turns the box around and examines the hinges at the back.

'Aida,' Spiros says again, and the other two turn to look at him.

'You what?' says Takis. Babis shrugs.

'Maybe we can borrow an angle grinder, and cut through the hinges with it. That might do it.'

The four letters form an image in Spiros's mind, but where has he seen them, and why does he have such a strong feeling that they are connected with the box? They were in another box, weren't they? No, not a box exactly – a case! And then it hits him, and he shouts the word aloud: 'Aida!'

Babis and Spiros stop talking now and turn to stare at him, but without any further explanation he is on his feet and hopping to the door. He hurries from the kitchen, kicks the coats away from the door, and, skipping and hopping, runs home as fast as he can.

Once inside, he pulls the briefcase from under his bed, pings the catches open, grabs the book in the waterproof bag and returns as fast as – if not faster than – he came.

Babis's door is still open; the lawyer and Takis are still sitting at the kitchen table, and they both look up, open-mouthed, at his return.

Spiros holds the book above his head as if it is a trophy.

'What have you got there?' Babis says.

'Oh, it's a book of George's,' Takis answers.

Babis seems none the wiser.

Spiros unzips the bag, takes out the book and slaps it onto the kitchen table, open at the first page.

Aida 1941 stares up at them.

'At first I thought it was a name and a date – but I think …'

He turns the box to face him.

'Let me.' Takis puts his hand out to take control.

'No!' Spiros snaps and Takis's hand withdraws.

Spiros turns the dial so it reads *1 – 9 – 4 – 1* and then, with shaking fingers, he lifts the lid. The box opens with no effort at all, and there, looking like something out of an action movie, are two solid bars of what can only be gold.

'Two!' Babis says, and his fingers wiggle in anticipation.

'They're not very big,' Takis says, and he takes one out. 'Wow, it's heavy.'

Spiros lifts the other bar. It fits in the palm of his hand, just. It is as thick as his little finger, but then he does have fat fingers. On its shiny surface are embossed numbers and shapes, none of which mean anything to him.

'Well, boys, congratulations,' Babis says. He cannot help himself, and he takes the bar from Takis, looks at it very closely.

'It's gold, right?' Takis asks.

'It's gold.' Babis smiles.

'Thank God for that,' Takis says.

'No, thank George,' Spiros replies.

'Well, boys, as your lawyer, I will do some research to discover their value, and find out who to sell to. Obviously it would have been easier if it was sovereigns, which are always being bought and sold … Gold bars, it may be a different matter.'

He reaches over to a pile of papers and pulls out a receipt book.

'You'll need to leave them with me so I can explain the markings and so on, but I reckon a couple of phone calls and I should have some idea.' He grins and starts to write.

'What are you doing?' Takis asks.

'Well, I would not have you leave these here without a receipt to say I have them. That is more than my reputation is worth,' he says cheerfully.

'Where are we going?' Spiros asks.

'I suggest you go and celebrate while I get the information we need. Here.' He rummages in the pocket of his jacket, which is hung over the chair next to him. 'Have an advance.' He hands a note to Takis. 'Get yourselves some breakfast and an ouzo chaser. You two look like you've been up all night!'

Takis takes the receipt.

'It has to be said, a good breakfast would do me the world of good,' he says, and he stands, rubbing his chest, his fingers drumming his ribcage.

'Come on, my friend,' he says to Spiros. 'I suggest a coffee and ouzo at Theo's and a slap-up breakfast at Stella's as soon as she is open – what do you say?'

Spiros cannot remember when he last ate, apart from the mints, of course, and besides, his head is spinning with the excitement of it all.

'Are we really rich?' he asks Babis.

'That there,' Babis says, pointing to the two bars, 'is solid gold and it is more than I expected. So yes, Spiro, I think it is fair to say that you are rich.'

'Come on, let's go celebrate!' Takis is suddenly animated, excited.

'It shouldn't take me more than a few hours at most to get some answers, so I'll catch you up either in the *kafenio* or at Stella's.'

They leave Babis, who is already on the phone to someone he knows in Athens and simultaneously on his computer, browsing the Internet.

Takis slaps Spiros on the back as they walk down into the square and across to Theo's, where the first farmers are already finishing their coffees before they set about their work.

'Theo, my man,' Takis says, 'two ouzos! Make them large ones.'

'Ouzo? At this time of day?' Theo wipes down his counter with a cloth.

'At this time of day!' Takis echoes, and he takes out the receipt for the gold. Before Spiros has any say in the matter, he slaps it on the counter in front of Theo. 'I, my friend, am a rich man.'

'Is that for real?' Theo takes it and turns it over, examining the paper closely.

'Call Babis if you don't believe me.'

'Have you had a bit of luck?' Mitsos is sitting at the nearest table with Cosmo the postman.

'Indeed I have! So in fact, Theo' – Takis takes the receipt and puts it back in his pocket – 'ouzo for everyone!'

The farmers fall silent for a fraction of a second and then call 'thanks,' and *'yeia mas'* to Takis.

'I think we should wait,' Spiros whispers.

'Why?' Takis says, not lowering his voice at all.

'I don't know, it just seems a bit–'

'That's your trouble, Spiro, you have no initiative, no spark, no adventure in you. Let's celebrate!'

Theo lines glasses up on the counter and pours from the bottle from one end of the line to the other. The farmers have all gathered round, eager to take their share of what is on offer. When they each have a glass, someone calls, *'Yeia mas!'* and it is echoed by every man in the room.

More farmers come in, wanting to know what is going on, and more ouzo is poured. Theo opens another bottle and then another and makes endless coffees, and he marks down the price of each on a piece of paper. There is soon a very long list of numbers. Not that Spiros would mind, if he had the cash in his hand. But as his mama has always said, only spend what you have in your pocket and then only if it is not needed somewhere else. He sips nervously on his ouzo and wonders if Theo could make him a milkshake.

The early morning drinkers become rowdy, and Takis keeps offering drinks and Theo keeps opening bottles. Spiros wonders when they will go for breakfast; he is very hungry. But Takis seems determined to stay awhile and so Spiros takes a seat by the window and watches the women of the village venturing to the corner shop with baskets over their arms and looking in at the *kafenio*, frowns knotting their eyebrows.

After an hour or so, the farmers settle down, the ouzo on empty stomachs catching up with them and making their limbs heavy. Takis joins him.

'To George,' he says, slurring his words and sitting heavily.

'Here comes Babis,' Spiros observes.

'Babi, have a drink!' Takis greets the lawyer.

But Babis is not smiling. He draws his chair in close to the table and leans over to them. 'Boys, I hope you've not spent more than the cash I gave you,' he says, looking around.

'But we are rich!' Takis slurs.

'Well, it seems we have a slight problem.'

'What!' Takis sounds suddenly sober.

'Well, it seems it is not legal to sell gold bars unless we have provenance.'

'What's provenance?' Spiros asks.

'Something to show where it came from, where it was bought, that it is legal.'

'And we don't have that?' Takis asks.

'No, we don't have that.'

'So what does that mean?' Spiros asks.

'It means the gold is worthless.' Babis sighs.

'Worthless!' Takis bellows, and just at that moment Theo puts a very large bill on the table.

If you enjoyed *The Village Idiots* please share it with a friend, and check out the other books in the Greek Village Collection!

I'm always delighted to receive email from readers, and I welcome new friends on Facebook.

https://www.facebook.com/authorsaraalexi

saraalexi@me.com

Happy reading,

Sara Alexi

Printed in Great Britain
by Amazon